Forc

The Old Sergeant, and Other Poems

SALZWASSER
VERLAG

Forceythe Willson

The Old Sergeant, and Other Poems

1st Edition | ISBN: 978-3-75257-562-0

Place of Publication: Frankfurt am Main, Germany

Year of Publication: 2022

Salzwasser Verlag GmbH, Germany.

Reprint of the original, first published in 1867.

THE
OLD SERGEANT,
AND OTHER POEMS.

BY

FORCEYTHE WILLSON.

BOSTON:
TICKNOR AND FIELDS.
1867.

Under the infinite arches
Of this Temple old and vast
Thou art come to Me at last.

The Mountains shall be thy step-stones,
Thy vestibule the Skies,
Unto all that beyond them lies.

CONTENTS.

THE OLD SERGEANT.

IN MEMORY

OF

THE IMMORTAL HEROES AND MARTYRS

OF

EMANCIPATION.

JAN. 1, 1863.

THE OLD SERGEANT.

JAN. 1, 1863.

THE Carrier cannot sing to-day the ballads
With which he used to go,
Rhyming the glad rounds of the happy New Years
That are now beneath the snow:

For the same awful and portentous Shadow
That overcast the earth,
And smote the land last year with desolation,
Still darkens every hearth.

And the carrier hears Beethoven's mighty death-
march
Come up from every mart;
And he hears and feels it breathing in his bosom,
And beating in his heart.

And to-day, a scarred and weather-beaten veteran,
    Again he comes along,
To tell the story of the Old Year's struggles
    In another New Year's song.

. .

And the song is his, but not so with the story;
    For the story, you must know,
Was told in prose to Assistant-Surgeon Austin,
    By a soldier of Shiloh:

By Robert Burton, who was brought up on the
        Adams,
    With his death-wound in his side;
And who told the story to the Assistant-Surgeon,
    On the same night that he died.

But the singer feels it will better suit the ballad,
    If all should deem it right,
To tell the story as if what it speaks of
    Had happened but last night.

"Come a little nearer, Doctor,—thank you,—let
me take the cup:
Draw your chair up,—draw it closer,—just another
little sup!
May be you may think I'm better; but I'm pretty
well used up,—
Doctor, you've done all you could do, but I'm
just a going up!

"Feel my pulse, sir, if you want to, but it ain't
much use to try"—
"Never say that," said the Surgeon, as he smothered
down a sigh;
"It will never do, old comrade, for a soldier to
say die!"
"What you *say* will make no difference, Doctor,
when you come to die."

"Doctor, what has been the matter?" "You were
very faint, they say;
You must try to get to sleep now." "Doctor,
have I been away?"
"Not that anybody knows of!" "Doctor — Doc-
tor, please to stay!
There is something I must tell you, and you won't
have long to stay!

"I have got my marching orders, and I'm ready
now to go;
Doctor, did you say I fainted? — but it could n't
ha' been so, —
For as sure as I'm a Sergeant, and was wounded at
Shiloh,
I've this very night been back there, on the old
field of Shiloh!

"This is all that I remember: The last time the
Lighter came,

And the lights had all been lowered, and the noises
much the same,
He had not been gone five minutes before something
called my name:
'ORDERLY SERGEANT — ROBERT BURTON!' — just
that way it called my name.

"And I wondered who could call me so distinctly
and so slow,
Knew it could n't be the Lighter, — he could not
have spoken so —
And I tried to answer, 'Here, sir!' but I could n't
make it go;
For I could n't move a muscle, and I could n't
make it go!

"Then I thought: It's all a nightmare, all a hum-
bug and a bore;
Just another foolish *grape-vine* * — and it won't
come any more;

* *Canard.*

"But it came, sir, notwithstanding, just the same way as before:
'ORDERLY SERGEANT — ROBERT BURTON!' — even plainer than before.

"That is all that I remember, till a sudden burst of light,
And I stood beside the River, where we stood that Sunday night,
Waiting to be ferried over to the dark bluffs opposite,
When the river was perdition and all hell was opposite! —

"And the same old palpitation came again in all its power,
And I heard a Bugle sounding, as from some celestial Tower;
And the same mysterious voice said: 'IT IS THE ELEVENTH HOUR!
ORDERLY SERGEANT — ROBERT BURTON — IT IS THE ELEVENTH HOUR!'

"Doctor Austin! — what *day* is this?" "It is
Wednesday night, you know."
"Yes, — to-morrow will be New Year's, and a right
good time below!
What *time* is it, Doctor Austin?" "Nearly Twelve."
"Then don't you go!
Can it be that all this happened — all this —
not an hour ago!

"There was where the gunboats opened on the dark
rebellious host;
And where Webster semicircled his last guns upon
the coast;
There were still the two log-houses, just the same,
or else their ghost, —
And the same old transport came and took me
over — or its ghost!

"And the old field lay before me all deserted far
and wide;
There was where they fell on Prentiss, — there Mc-
Clernand met the tide;

There was where stern Sherman rallied, and where
Hurlbut's heroes died, —
Lower down, where Wallace charged them, and
kept charging till he died.

"There was where Lew Wallace showed them he
was of the canny kin,
There was where old Nelson thundered, and where
Rousseau waded in;
There McCook sent 'em to breakfast, and we all be-
gan to win —
There was where the grape-shot took me, just as
we began to win.

"Now, a shroud of snow and silence over everything
was spread;
And but for this old blue mantle and the old hat
on my head,
I should not have even doubted, to this moment, I
was dead, —
For my footsteps were as silent as the snow upon
the dead!

"Death and silence!—Death and silence! all around
me as I sped!
And behold, a mighty TOWER, as if builded to the
dead,—
To the Heaven of the heavens, lifted up its mighty
head,
Till the Stars and Stripes of Heaven all seemed
waving from its head!

"Round and mighty-based it towered—up into the
infinite—
And I knew no mortal mason could have built a shaft
so bright;
For it shone like solid sunshine; and a winding
stair of light,
Wound around it and around it till it wound clear
out of sight!

"And, behold, as I approached it—with a rapt and
dazzled stare,—
Thinking that I saw old comrades just ascending
the great Stair,—

Suddenly the solemn challenge broke of — 'Halt, and who goes there!'
'I'm a friend,' I said, 'if you are.' — 'Then advance, sir, to the Stair!'

"I advanced! — That sentry, Doctor, was Elijah Ballantyne! —
First of all to fall on Monday, after we had formed the line! —
'Welcome, my old Sergeant, welcome! Welcome by that countersign!'
And he pointed to the scar there, under this old cloak of mine!

"As he grasped my hand, I shuddered, thinking only of the grave;
But he smiled and pointed upward with a bright and bloodless glaive:
'That 's the way, sir, to Head-quarters.' 'What Head-quarters!' — 'Of the Brave.'
But the great Tower?' — 'That,' he answered, 'Is the way, sir, of the Brave!'

"Then a sudden shame came o'er me at his uniform
of light;
At my own so old and tattered, and at his so new
and bright;
'Ah!' said he, 'you have forgotten the New Uni-
form to-night, —
Hurry back, for you must be here at just twelve
o'clock to-night!'

"And the next thing I remember, you were sitting
there, and I —
Doctor — did you hear a footstep? Hark! — God
bless you all! Good by!
Doctor, please to give my musket and my knap-
sack, when I die,
To my Son — my Son that s coming, — he won't
get here till I die!

"Tell him his old father blessed him as he never
did before, —
And to carry that old musket" — Hark! a knock is
at the door! —

"Till the Union—" See! it opens!—"Father!
Father! speak once more!"—
"*Bless you!*"—gasped the old, gray Sergeant,
And he lay and said no more!

ARPEGGIOS.

THE MYSTIC THOUGHT.

THERE came a Mystic Thought to me;
  If any soul should ask me, "Whence?"
I can but say, I could not see,
  Nor hear nor feel, in any sense.
As the glory of the rising moon
Is duplicated in the lagoon,
Or gleams on the old tower and its spire,
Till the cross becomes a cross of fire, —
So that strange Thought, serene and lone,
Rose on my dark soul, and it shone!

Shouldst ask me, if an Angel brought
This strange, this sweet and secret Thought?
I could but say, I do not know!
It came as comes the guiding glow

From Heaven's high shrines; or as the snow
On the dark hill-tops; or as bloom
  The intimations of a God
In every violet of the tomb,
  And every pansy of the sod.

It came, unbidden, — as it went, —
A wingéd, wandering Sentiment,
That for a moment fanned my lyre
With passing wings, of faint, white fire:
Five finger-tips were touched to mine,
Most lightly: and a drop of wine,
Or dew, fell on my lips. At last,
A breath, — a seeming kiss —
                it passed!

THE DELL.

Two Poets live and work at will
  In the highlands by the river-sheen :
One hath his harp and domicile
Up on the sun-kindled, wind-kissed hill ;
And one, his shrine somewhere in the still,
Divinely tenanted secrecy of the inviolable ravine.

He, the Young Poet, who exults
  Up on the hill-top, all alone ;
And feels along his veins the pulse
  Of Nature stronger than his own ;
His subtle thought and sacred chime
Have caught and charmed the ear of Time ;
His name and fair-found fellowship
Are honored on the living lip.

But the Old Poet, who hath wreaked
  The spirit of his ancient spell
On the rugged granite scarped and peaked,
  Down in the shadow of the Dell, —
There is no servitor to show
The pilgrim to his portico.

No voice is ever audible
With "Welcome and thrice welcome, sire!"
However just and laudable
    The motive of the visitor;
No jarring of a vexéd lyre
With, "Hark ye, sirrah, go thy way!"
    To awe an uncouth quisitor
For trespass or for overstay.

But should some churl, eschewed of grace,
Shew there his melancholy face,

And biting his curled lip exclaim :
" Ye gods, why did ye make the place ?
An utter waste, — It is a shame ! —
A mere chance causey, through and through,
— Could come of nothing but misrule!
Tut, tut, poor rocks, I pity you,
The Master here must be a fool ! "
The Rock would answer deep and cool:
" *I pity you — I pity you —*
The Master here must be a fool."

But should the heaven-loved Elinor,
Who bideth but a little while
Ere we shall clasp her hand no more,
Kneel down in secret there and pray,
With her last breath and dying smile,
" Dear Spirit, come to me to-day ! "
A Voice within, perchance, might say :
" *Dear Spirit, come to me to-day.*"

And in that Dell there is no tree,
No leaf nor flower, no bird nor bee,
  No lifeless, and no living thing,
  But feels the fine forefingering
Of his inimitable fantasy;
  Is there, no rivulet nor stream,
  No earth-born shade nor heaven-born beam,
But hath some slight, especial part
  In the romantic work and dream
Of this Old Poet's mind and heart.

The merest animated mite
  That revelled in his tiny rings
Ten thousand years ago to-night,
And was so whimsically slight,
  He never knew the need of wings;
But rose in ecstasy with light,
And shed his little overplight
Of mortal ashes in one flight;
  The busy-footed centipede,

That crept his native leaflet's rim,
Till he wore off from every limb
  His birth-woof, with instinctive speed,
  And ran regenerate up the reed, —
  Had instinct of the Poet's need,
And kept fine harmony with him:
  And all, according to their meed,
Are there embalmed, forevermore, amid his cryptographic tomes.

"AND THE BEAUTIFUL, IN HER FAINTNESS, SMILED."

The Beautiful lived in the Land of the Blest,
By the Beautiful River that winds to the West,
Through the Valley that True Love loves the best.

But she did not live in a castle-tower,
Nor yet on a throne; but like a flower,
With the infinite canopy for her bower.

And under her leafy balcony,
At a lattice dear to the honey-bee,
And the humming-bird, — was a Tulip-tree.

And among its leaves was the hidden nest,
Of a Wonderful Bird with a luminous crest,
And the dew and the blue on its wings and breast:

And there at the lattice, and all alone,
The strange Bird sang in a low, sweet tone,
As a soul doth to itself make moan!

And the first that ever the Beautiful heard
Of its plaintive lay, she loved the bird,
For her heart was touched, and her soul was stirred.

And as soon as the day had gone to rest,
She always arose with the Star in the West,
And opened her casement to the nest.

Then from the leafy aureole
Of the Tulip-tree a sweet strain stole,
And kissed to sleep her white-robed soul!

And the Beautiful was beatified,
And blushed in her dream like a bashful bride,
When her heart's Heart first beats at her side.

For she dreamed . . . that her lone guest,
With the heavenly music in its breast,
Was the Soul that, of all souls, loved her best.

And the rapturous heart-warmth of the rose,
Seemed to blend with the purity of the snows,
In the perfect sweetness of her repose.

— But once, as the night rose to depart,
The Beautiful woke with a sudden start,
And a fluttering, as it were, in her heart;

And she put forth her hands in wistful quest,
And a Living Wonder lay on her breast,
That had just fluttered down, as it were, from the nest!

And the Beautiful, in her faintness, smiled.

THE DEW-DROP.

Fairy fingers always pluck
Sprigs of spring for summer luck, —
Leaf, and slip, and clover-head,
No bee hath o'er-hoveréd, —
The dew upon the clover-top
Must tremble, but it must not drop!

For when the bats begin to flit,
And the glimmering lawns are lit
Momently with a fire-fly light,
Thro' the lattice of twilight,
Tiny fingers of moonshine
With my lute-strings intertwine!

Moonshine-fingers, winter-clear,
With my lute-strings interfere!
Fairies bring the clover-top,
And shake down the sweet Dew-Drop;
It lights and trembles on my lips,
And thus into a song it slips:

Marry, in the moonlight, marry, O marry!
The lily-queen trembles and leans to the lily
Which for the love of her grows nearest!
Whispering, "Wake Willie, wake Willie, wake Willie,
Breath o' my life, Willie,
Willie my dearest!

Marry, in the moonlight, marry, O marry,
The sweetest is given, and given and taken!
Queenly Beloved, thou art the nearest;
And Willie is a-waiting for you to awaken!
Awaiting — awaiting —
For you to awaken!

IN THE DARK.

Hush — was there anything in the dark —
Like a whisper or cry in the dark?
"O Darling — my Darling," were the words that seemed
To be breathed in my ear! — but I must have dreamed!
It was only a dream I know, — but hark!
Is there anything, anything more in the dark?

"O Darling — my Darling" — again in the dark!
As it used to be in the dark!
And fingers of spirit-like tenderness
Are intertwined lovingly with my tress;
I know it is only a dream — but hark!
Is there anything, anything more in the dark?

"O Darling!" — again and again in the dark!
Like a whisper of love in the dark!
And then, as of old, his brave arm seems
To fold me up in his loving dreams:
I know that it never will be, — but hark!
Is there anything, anything more in the dark?

Ah — yes! there is something more in the dark,
There is something more in the dark!
All alone In The Dark am I,
And sick unto death — but I cannot die!
And I must not die! — but hark, O hark!
Is there anything, anything more in the dark?

Yes! Now, there is something more, In The Dark!
There is something more, now, In The Dark!
Here in my bosom it pleads: "Don't die:"
A "miniature"? — Yes, and a little cry!
A little forlorn and forsaken Spark,
That will soon go out in the Rain and the Dark!

O come to me! Come to me! here In The Dark!
As you used to, you know — in the dark!
And call me your "dear little wife" once more,
Just as you did in the days of yore!
And kiss me! And bless me! And oh!—but hark!
There is nothing more — nothing more — In The
Dark!

THE ESTRAY.

" Now tell me, my merry woodman,
 Why standest so aghast ? "
" My lord ! — 't was a beautiful creature
 That hath but just gone past ! "

" A creature — what kind of a creature ? "
 " Nay now, but I do not know ! "
" Humph — what did it make you think of ? "
 " The sunshine on the snow."

" I shall overtake my horse then : "
 The woodman opened his eye : —
The gold fell all around him,
 And a rainbow spanned the sky.

THE APOTHEOSIS OF APOLLO.

"I WILL follow thee, follow thee, follow thee,
With the god-speed of Endeavor;
Till thou wholly yieldest up to me
The elixir and the ecstasy
Of thy Love and thine Immortality,
And crownest me forever!"

And the Poet sped, sped, sped,
To the foot of the Heavenly Mountain,
With the Sunshine's prance and the Lightning's tread;
And the sword-flash of his Soul smote dead
The terrible Dragon The Beautiful bred
To guard her Sacred Fountain!

To the Bath — whence even the gods are kept
For ever and ever banished, —
In the passionate speed of his soul he swept;
But into the Fountain the Goddess leaped,
And mingled and mounted, and smiled and wept,
In a rainbow as she vanished!

"But ho! by the gods," he cried and lo,
And into the Bath he bounded!
And flinging his mantle off into the flow,
Rose pure, and swift and pure — ho! ho! —
As a shaft of light from the beautiful Bow,
Into the clouds he mounted

Into the clouds — ho! ho! —
And into her bower he darted;
But the clouds dissolved with a golden glow,
That gilded the Mountain's crown below;
And the rain fell blossoming into snow,
And The Beautiful had departed.

Had slid, slid up, with a sunbeam's sleight,
    And with the sunbeams blended, —
Had glided up like the light of light,
Through the misty abysses of Death and Night,
To the Fountain-head of Divine Delight,
    And into the sun ascended!

But swifter than all that darts or gleams,
    Was the Poet's rapt endeavor;
And up from the world, and its cloudy schemes,
He flashed to the Sun in his deathless dreams;
And The Beautiful crowned him with the beams
    Of her Glory and Love forever!

DIANA OF THE HUNT.

All can see, in the shining places,
Vestiges of her classic graces;
Where her footsteps, fleet and stark,
Have beautifully embossed the dark.

We know indeed, that the stately and golden
Antlers, hunters and heroes olden,
Wood-nymph, satyr, and sylvan faun, —
Goddess and stag, are gone! — all gone!

But still, — as strange as it may appear, —
Sometimes when the nights are bright and clear,
The long-breathed hounds are heard to bay
Over the hills and far away!

And lovers who walk at Love's high Noon,
See something flash in the light of the moon,
As a shining stag swept through the sky,
And the chase of the goddess were up, on high.

But be this as it may, in sooth,
It is only in the pursuit of Truth,
That the Soul shall overtake and possess
The most exalted Happiness.

TO HERSA.

MAIDEN, there is something more
Than raiment to adore:
Thou must have more than a dress,
More than any mode or mould,
More than mortal loveliness,
To captivate the cold.

Bow the knightly when they bow,
To a star behind the brow:
Not to marble, not to dust;
  But to that which warms them:
Not to contour nor to bust;
  But to that which forms them:
Not to languid lid nor lash,
Satin fold nor purple sash;
But unto the living flash

So mysteriously hid
Under lash and under lid.

But — vanity of vanities, —
If the red-rose in a young cheek, lies,
    Fatal disguise!
For the most terrible lances
Of the True, true Knight,
Are his bold eyebeams;
And every time that he opens his eyes,
The Falsehood that he looks on, dies.

If the heavenly light be latent,
It can need no earthly patent.
    Unbeholden unto art,
    Fashion or lore,
    Scrip or store,
    Earth or ore,
    Be thy heart,
Which was music from the start,
Music, music to the core.

Music, which, though voiceless,
Can create
Both form and fate,
As Petrarch could a sonnet.
That, taking flesh upon it,
Spirit-noiseless,
Doth the same inform and fill
With a Music sweeter still, —
Lives, and breathes, and palpitates,
Moves, and moulds, and animates,
And sleeps not from its duty
Till the maid in whom 't is pent,
From a mortal rudiment,
From the earth-cell
  And the love-cell
By the birth-spell
  And the love-spell,
Come to beauty.

Beauty is music mute,
Music's flower and fruit,

Music's lute:
Music's lute be thou,
Maiden of the starry brow,
(Keep thy heart true to know how!)
A Lute which he alone,
As all in good time shall be shown,
Shall prove and thereby make his own,
Who is god enough to play upon it.

Happy, happy maid is she
Who is wedded unto Truth!
Thou shalt know him, when he comes,
(Welcome youth!)
Not by any din of drums,
Nor the vantage of his airs;
Neither by his crown,
Nor his gown,
Nor by anything he wears.
He shall only well-known be,
By the holy Harmony
That his coming makes in thee!

SPHERE-SONG.

Once upon a time,
Through the crevice of mine ear,
The Music of the Sphere
Ran into rhyme :

" Wouldst possess the starry treasure,
Elixir of Life and Pleasure ?

" Only Truth is never olden,
Truth alone is ever golden.

" On whatever plain thou pitchest,
E'en the True man is the richest.

"And of all for whom thou waitest,
Aye the True man is the greatest.

"But, as most of all behooveth,
He alone is Good who Loveth:

"And however false man proveth,
He alone is True who Loveth:

"Who loves earliest, best, and latest,
Is the richest, best, and greatest!"

Then again all was at rest,
In mine ear;
Till I cried: "O Sphere!
Who of all men loveth best?"

Then the Sphere resounded farther:
"True King Alfred, True Knight Arthur!

"He that loveth like a lover
All that sin and all that suffer:

"He that loves all forms and features,
All creations and all creatures:

"Loves all souls, and spheres, and spaces;
Loves all regions and all races:

"Yet so loveth nothing finite,
But to God he can resign it:

"Living greatly for the Whole-sake,
Greatly suffering for the Soul-sake:

"Drawing all with true Endeavor,
To his heart of hearts forever."

And lo, as I heard the last rhymes play,
The bird that is most like a bee hove near, —
Hummed the *finalé* in mine ear,
And whizzed away.

THE RHYME
OF
THE MASTER'S MATE.

There was something, perhaps, the Master knew
Far better than we for his Mate to do.

PRELUDE.

THE long roll of the drum and the last lonesome echo
Of the Bugle's long-breathed lay,
Like a mighty soul in the chariot of his triumph,
Hath gone its heavenward way.

And a solemn hush, a deep and world-wide silence,
Broods on the strife at last;
The armaments that shook the world beneath them
Dissolve into the Past.

Like the vast enginery of some appalling Vision
Of World-wreck and Despair,
Dissolve with slow, eclipse-like, dread transition,
Into the infinite air!

And leave to greet the astonished gaze of nations,
As by the quake upheaved,
The fairest Land that Freedom ever smiled on,
Or Fantasy conceived!

A Land wherein, by grace of the God of Heaven,
And the Memory of the Brave,
No man shall henceforth dare to be a traitor,
Nor brook to be a slave!

THE RHYME OF THE MASTER'S MATE.

FORT HENRY.

None who saw it can forget
How they went into the fight,
Four abreast, —
Thereby was the foe perplexed, —
With the Essex on the right,
That is nearest to the Fort —
And the Cincinnati next,
The St. Louis on her left,
All so gallant and so deft —
And the brave Carondelet.

Boom! boom! from every bow:
(They 'll have to answer that!)

From the Rebel bastions, now,
        There 's a flash.
Cool, keep cool, boys, — don't be rash;
Mind your eyes, as the old Boss said;
Keep together and go ahead, —
Not too high and not too low,
        Fire slow!

        Paff!
Now we have it from the Fort,
And the Rebels all a-crowing!
While the devils'-echoes laugh,
With a loonish thunder-lowing,
After every gun's report:
'T is n't bird-shot they are throwing,
        'T is n't chaff!

        Ping! Ping!
If you 've ever seen the thing
That can fly without a wing

Swifter than the Thunder's bird,
Lightning-clenching, lightning-spurred,
If you 've ever heard it sing, —
You will understand the word,
And look out;
For beyond a mortal doubt,
It can sting!

Thump!
'D y' ever hear anything like it?
Sounded very much like a ten-strike — it
Appears they 're after a spare!
Bet it made the old Boss jump,
Or at any rate awfully screw up his brows,
Hit the pilot-house, —
And he 's up there, —
Must 'a' been a hundred-pounder,
Had the twang of a conical ball,
Would 'a' gone plumb through a ten-foot wall.
Is n't the old *Cinc* a trump?

They meant that for a damper!
Square it off with an eighty shell
And a fifteen-second fuse,
(With all the latest news!) —
Pretty well done, boys — pretty well!
Guess that'll be apt to tell
'Em all about where it came from,
And where it's a-going to, —
What it took its name from,
And all it's a-knowing to!
See 'em scamper!

The Conestoga, the Tyler,
And the Lexington, you know,
Are in line a half a mile, or
A little less, below,
Just this side of the Panther
(Little woody island).
They've their orders —— Oh!
But, after all, how *can* their

Wooden-heads keep silent?
Wonder 'f it don't make 'em feel bad,
Even if they ain't all *steel*-clad,
At being slighted so!

'T is n't so bad a day,
Although it 's a little cloudy;
Or rather, as one might say,
Smoky, perhaps, —
A little hazy, a little dubious,
A little too sulphury to be salubrious!
D' ye mind those thunder-claps?
Do you feel now and then the least little bit
Of an incipient earthquake fit?
Accompanied with awful raps?
But give 'em gowdy! give 'em gowdy!
And it 'll soon clear away!

Old Boss ain't to be balked! —
All this, you know,

Was only the way (or nearly so)
The boys talked,
And felt and thought, —
And acted, too, —
The harder they fought
And the hotter it grew.

But there was a Hand at the reel
That nobody saw!
Old Hickory there at every keel,
In every timber, from stem to stern!
A *something* — in every crank and wheel,
That made 'em answer their turn!
And everywhere,
On earth and water, in fire and air,
As it were to see it all well done,
The Wraith of the murdered Law —
Old John Brown at every gun!

But the Fort was all in a roar:
No use to talk, they had the range, —

Which was n't strange, —
Guess they 'd tried it before ! —
And the pounding was not soft,
But might well appall
The boldest heart.
Cool and calm,
Trumpet in hand,
Up in the cock-loft,
Where 't was the hottest of all,
Our brave old Commodore
Took his stand,
And played his part,
Humming over some old psalm !

Tut ! did ye hear the hiss and scream
Of that hot steam ?
It 's the Essex that 's struck, —
She never had any luck :
Ah ! 't was a wicked shot,
And, whether they know it or not,

It does n't give us joy!
Thorough an open port it flew,
As with some special permit to destroy;
And first, for sport,
Struck the soul from that beautiful boy;
Then through the bulkhead lunged,
And into the boiler plunged,
Scalding the whole crew!

We know that the brave must fall,
But that was a sight to see:
Twenty-three,
All in an instant scalded and scathed,
All at once in the white shroud swathed!
A low moan came from the deck
Of the drifting wreck, —
And that was all.

How the traitors 'll boast,
As soon as they come to see her

All adrift and aghast!
Hark! d' ye hear? d' ye hear?
D' ye hear 'em shout?
They see it already, no doubt.
We shall have to count her out, —
That white breath was her last, —
She has given up the ghost!

What does the old Boss think?
Will he shrink?
Will he waver or falter now?
A little shadow flits over his brow,
For the sharp pang in his heart:
Flits over — and is gone!
And a light looms up in his old gray eye.
Whether you see it or not,
That is like a sudden dawn
In a stormy sky!

What does he *think*? —
What will he *do*?

Well! he don't say!
But I 'll tell you what,
  You can bet your life,
As you would your knife,
(And your wife, too,)
      He 'll do,
And put 'em up at once:
He 'll run these boats right up to their guns,
  And take that Fort, or sink!

But, oh — oh, it was hot!
So thick and fast the solid shot
Upon our iron armor played,
It kept, like thunder, a kind of time, —
Devil's tattoo or gallopade, —
That, like an awful, awful rhyme,
      Rang in the ear;
And they sent us cheer after cheer.

But the boys had been to *school*,
And *their* guns were not cool!

For they knew what Cause they served,
And not a man of 'em swerved!
But on, right on, they swept,
And from every grim bow-port
Their nutmegs and shell-barks leaped
  Into the jaws of the Fort!
And (to give her, perhaps, a chance to breathe)
Knocked out some of her big, black teeth!
And (to raise a better crop, no doubt,
Than was ever raised there before)
Ploughed her up into awful creases, —
      Inside and out! —
For now they were up and doing the chore
At only four hundred yards,
And the death-dealing shreds and shards
Of our shell were tearing 'em all to pieces!

  Hurrah for the brave old Flag!
To triumph see her ride! —
Ha, ha! they dodge and duck!

The Snake 's expiring, —
Their gunners run and hide!
By heaven, they 've struck!
Down comes the rattlesnake rag
By the run, —
Stop the firing!
The work is done!

— Anyhow, she 'll do for batter!
You see now, Butternuts, you were plucky;
But that ain't "what 's the matter," —
Not by a long shot!
No, no, — no! I 'll tell you what —
And you must n't take it at all amiss —
I 'll tell you what the *matter* is:
'T ain't because you were born unlucky,
(Bear in mind,)
Nor that you 've good eyes and we are blind, —
Nothing of the kind!

But it 's something else, if it is n't more :
The reason — pardon ! — you had to cotton
Was simply this :
☞ Your *Cause* was rotten :
Rotten to the very core :
That 's " what 's the matter ! "

But you ought to 'a' heard our water-dogs yelp ! —
Just an hour and fifteen minutes ! —
(Twitter away, you English linnets !)
Horizontal and perpendicular,
Fair and square, without any help, —
That is, any in particular, —
The old ferry wash-tubs of the West
With some new-fashioned *hoops,* — for a little test,
And a few old *pounders* from — Kingdom Come,
And nothing for suds but the — *Nawth'n scum,*
Made these " gen'l'men " turn as white
As a head o' hair in a single night !
Cleaned their army completely out,

(We 're going to give *that* another wipe!)
On the double-quick, by the shortest route:
Wrung their stronghold from their gripe,
Brought their garrison right to taw,
And made 'em get down to the "higher law"!

So that when Grant and his boys came up, —
There 's places enough for a man to die! —
Swearing that we had "*spiled*" the "sport,"
With a quiet twinkle in his eye,
Old Boss asked 'em to come in and sup,
And set 'em to *house-keeping* — in the Fort! —
But all the old fellow could say or do,
They 'd still keep a-going it: "*Bully for you!*"

Bully for Grant and for Foote!
E'en if the voice must tremble:
And *Bully* for all who helped 'em to do 't!
Bully for Porter and Stemble!
For Paulding and for Walke, —

For Phelps, for Gwin, and for Shirk!
But what 's the use to talk? —
They were all of 'em up to the work!
  Bully for each brave tub
That bore the Union Blue!
And for every mother's son
Of every gallant crew,
Whatever his color or name,
Who — when it came to the rub —
Shall be found to have been — *game!*

Such was the Rhyme of the Master's Mate,
Just as they found it in the locker,
With this at the foot:
        "It 's getting late,
And I hear a pretty loud Knock at the knocker!
Captain, if I should chance to fall,
Try to send me home. Good bye!" That 's all,
Excepting the date, the name, and rank:
  "Feb. 12th, '62, —— ——,
        Master's Mate."

Three days after, at rise of sun,
Just below Fort Donelson,
On the Cumberland River lay a wreck:
And the Captain stood again,
Upon his deck,
And to the living said:
"Wrap him in the ship's flag, men!"

IN STATE.

I.

O Keeper of the Sacred Key,
And the Great Seal of Destiny,
Whose eye is the blue canopy,
Look down upon the warring world, and tell us what
the end will be.

"Lo, through the wintry atmosphere,
On the white bosom of the sphere,
A cluster of five lakes appear;
And all the land looks like a couch, or warrior's
shield, or sheeted bier.

"And on that vast and hollow field,
With both lips closed and both eyes sealed,
A mighty Figure is revealed, —
Stretched at full length, and stiff and stark,
as in the hollow of a shield.

"The winds have tied the drifted snow
Around the face and chin ; and lo,
The sceptred Giants come and go,
And shake their shadowy crowns and say : "We always feared it would be so!"

"She came of an heroic race :
A giant's strength, a maiden's grace,
Like two in one seem to embrace,
And match, and blend, and thorough-blend, in her colossal form and face.

"Where can her dazzling falchion be?
One hand is fallen in the sea ;
The Gulf-Stream drifts it far and free ;
And in that hand her shining brand gleams from the depths resplendently.

"And by the other, in its rest,
The starry banner of the West

Is clasped forever to her breast;
And of her silver helmet, lo, a soaring eagle is the
crest.

"And on her brow, a softened light,
As of a star concealed from sight
By some thin veil of fleecy white, —
Or of the rising moon behind the rainy vapors of the
night.

"The Sisterhood that was so sweet,
The Starry System sphered complete,
Which the mazed Orient used to greet,
The Four and Thirty fallen Stars glimmer and glitter
at her feet.

"And over her, — and over all,
For panoply and coronal, —
The mighty Immemorial,
And everlasting Canopy and starry Arch and Shield
of All."

II.

"Three cold, bright moons have marched and wheeled;
And the white cerement that revealed
A Figure stretched upon a Shield,
Is turned to verdure; and the Land is now one mighty Battle-Field.

"And lo, the children which she bred,
And more than all else cherishéd,
To make them true in heart and head,
Stand face to face, as mortal foes, with their swords crossed above the dead.

"Each hath a mighty stroke and stride:
One true — the more that he is tried;
The other dark and evil-eyed; —
And by the hand of one of them, his own dear mother surely died!

"A stealthy step — a gleam of hell, —
It is the simple truth to tell, —
The Son stabbed and the Mother fell:
And so she lies, all mute and pale, and pure and irreproachable!

"And then the battle-trumpet blew;
And the true brother sprang and drew
His blade to smite the traitor through;
And so they clashed above the bier, and the Night sweated bloody dew.

"And all their children, far and wide,
That are so greatly multiplied,
Rise up in frensy and divide;
And choosing, each whom he will serve, unsheathe the sword and take their side.

"And in the low sun's bloodshot rays,
Portentous of the coming days,

The Two great Oceans blush and blaze,
With the emergent continent between them, wrapt
in crimson haze.

"Now whichsoever stand or fall,
As God is great and man is small,
The Truth shall triumph over all, —
Forever and forevermore, the Truth shall triumph
over all!"

III.

"I SEE the champion sword-strokes flash;
I see them fall and hear them clash;
I hear the murderous engines crash;
I see a brother stoop to loose a foeman-brother's
bloody sash.

"I see the torn and mangled corse,
The dead and dying heaped in scores,

The headless rider by his horse,
The wounded captive bayoneted through and through
without remorse.

"I hear the dying sufferer cry,
With his crushed face turned to the sky,
I see him crawl in agony
To the foul pool, and bow his head into its bloody
slime and die.

"I see the assassin crouch and fire,
I see his victim fall — expire;
I see the murderer creeping nigher
To strip the dead: He turns the head: The face!
The son beholds his sire!

"I hear the curses and the thanks;
I see the mad charge on the flanks,
The rents — the gaps — the broken ranks, —
The vanquished squadrons driven headlong down the
river's bridgeless banks.

"I see the death-gripe on the plain,
The grappling monsters on the main,
The tens of thousands that are slain,
And all the speechless suffering and agony of heart
and brain.

"I see the dark and bloody spots,
The crowded rooms and crowded cots,
The bleaching bones, the battle-blots, —
And writ on many a nameless grave, a legend of
forget-me-nots.

"I see the gorgéd prison-den,
The dead line and the pent-up pen,
The thousands quartered in the fen,
The living-deaths of skin and bone that were the
goodly shapes of men.

"And still the bloody Dew must fall!
And His great Darkness with the Pall

Of His dread Judgment cover all,
Till the Dead Nation rise Transformed by Truth to
triumph over all!"

"AND LAST — AND LAST I SEE — THE DEED."

Thus saith the Keeper of the Key,
And the Great Seal of Destiny,
Whose Eye is the blue canopy,
And leaves the Pall of His great Darkness over all
the Land and Sea.

EMANCIPATION HYMN.

O DID ye hear
That Clarion clear
That sounded over land and sea?
"Absolve the ban
Of Canäan:"
It was the Trump of Jubilee!

Lo, as of old,
Again behold,
The waves divide amidst the sea!
Again thy rod
Prevails, O God,
And turns the tide to Jubilee!

Thy Cloud by day
Still leads the way;
And flaming back across the sea,
Thro' Dark and Dire,
Thy Pillared Fire,
The beacon-blaze of Jubilee!

Thou lettest, Lord,
Thy Living Word
Again go forth from sea to sea:
"ABSOLVE THE BAN
THAT FETTERS MAN:
PROCLAIM, PROCLAIM THE JUBILEE!"

ECCE SIGNUM.

To the Westward the wild ruins of the Tempest roll
away;
And the pomp of sunset closes the long tumult of
the day.

Softly thrown back from her tresses floats the wingéd
mantle-mist;
One foot on the land is resting, — one is by the billows kissed.

All the Kingdoms and their creatures are extended
round her seat;
And a Vessel, like a child's-toy rides and dances
at her feet.

Rising over her left shoulder the moon waxes to her
will;
And the Day's departing footsteps glorify the mountains still.

Rests a white dove in her bosom, with an olive-branch of balm;
And The heavenly Bow of Promise consecrates her
brows to calm.

O the deep repose and beauty of that form who may
declare,
As revealed through the transparent drapery of the
twilight air!

The last light is on her forehead: at her feet the
darkness cowers:
She is gazing towards the sunset, and her lap is full
of flowers.

And a more than mortal Pathos over all her face is
cast,
As if she were gazing backward upon all that which
is past.

And a Light that is not sunlight, hovers round her
lips the while,
Like the tender and prophetic intimation of a smile.

As if she were gazing forward through the sacred
Mystery
Of the Infinite Hereafter and of all that is To Be.

And enraptured by the grandeur of the Vision that
she saw,
And transfigured in its glory, could but gaze in
silent awe!

THE CHURCH.

One little group was kneeling far down the silent
nave,
As in the very Valley and deep Shadow of the
Grave.

Then a sound low as the accents heard when little
children pray,
Struggled up into the silence, and in silence died
away.

Tones of deep and holy Passion, as for some abiding
Loss,
Rising now above the Altar, seemed to hover round
the Cross.

Then the interval was broken with a burst of thunder tones!
And the Music shook the Temple to its foundation stones!

Then methought: "Again the Samson wrestles with the heathen walls";
And I heard above the tumult cried, "The House of Dagon falls!"

And I saw the walls and columns rock and totter to and fro,
Till they toppled down and thundered into the abyss below!

But the little group — behold it! — all unscathed amidst the shock,
Kneeling in the open sunshine, on the Everlasting Rock!

A VALEDICTORY.

THE Infinite fills one and all :
The little animated mote,
That on a rose's breath might float,
Or on a sunbeam rise and doat,
God liveth in him, still and small.

Wherefore the earth in eld began,
And God in ancient darkness wrought :
That matter might, at length, be brought
To palpitate with Life and Thought,
And take in Thee the mould of Man.

Incalculable epochs past,
The Void hath filled, the Vague hath cleared,
The orbs, in music, matched and sphered,

Till in its orbit earth appeared,
    And, out of earth, Thyself, at last.

    "Thou art of too Divine a Birth,"
The conscious Soul within thee saith,
"To think the Second-Birth, called Death,
Can quench thine Inner pulse and breath,
    Or down-dissolve thee into earth":

    "For all the members intimate,
By signs of growth that are as clear
As any music to the ear,
That thou art merely passing here
    Through a prelusive phase or state:

    "And that, within thee, something swims,
Of which thy body is the sign,
Whereof a good eye can divine
A taking-shape, a mystic shine,
    And the glimmer of immortal limbs.

"As in a puck-etched acorn-cup,
A searching soul can clearly see
The forethought and epitome
Of that majestic Forest-Tree,
Which from it surely shall come up.

"Nor can one urge that, inasmuch,
As in some coming century,
The Oak shall fall, and so shall lie,
That so, in sooth, must thou and I,
And Man and Tree be such and such:

"The Tree falls, but it lieth, not:
Five hundred years be past and lo,
What is there of it left to show?
The Tree is gone: Where did it go?
The Vanished Tree replieth not.

"The Tree falls, but it lieth not:
Where once it stood — alone perchance,

The family of the forest stands;
Or the monster of the million-hands, —
The Vanished Tree replieth not!

"The Trunk that long outbraved the storms,
Hath doubtless entered other forms;
The Living Spirit of the Tree
Dissolved forevermore may be:
But why should that discourage Thee?

"All animated as thou art,
By that inherent Man of Fire,
That gives thee Life and its desire,
And all thy power to aspire
Unto a better life and heart, —

"Thou shalt not render to distrust
A moment's tribute! But shalt give
Thyself assurance that To Live,
Is a godlike prerogative;
To Die, — but to shake off the dust!

"As well, in sooth, tear-blur the eye,
And pass the summer morn in dole,
Over the cast-off husk or poll
Of some old symbol of the Soul —
The swaddle of the butterfly:

"While near at hand the very while,
Her little dross-divested sprite
Spreads wings like Psyche, for a flight
Into illimitable light,
To revel in the Summer's smile.

"Behold thy little daughter, Grace:
Lo, canst thou not identify
Thyself in her as verily,
As in the love-blue of her eye
The mirrored image of thy face?

"For all thou ever wast, before
Her speechless smile blessed thee for thine,

With mother-grace did intertwine,
An endless with an endless line,
　　To live through her forevermore!

　　"Nor only in thy seed thy soul
Shall thrid the cycles: But above,
Through ways and worlds thou know'st not of,
Thou shalt, thyself, be led by Love,
　　To some conception of the Whole.

　　"And thou wilt find, from first to last,
Through all thy varying career,
In passing on from sphere to sphere,
Thou only, livest, — Now and Here, —
　　In that one moment which thou hast.

　　"And that in knowing Nature's needs,
Through thy great-hearted sympathy,
With God and with Humanity,
Thou hast an Immortality,
　　To consecrate to noble deeds."

THE POET'S EPILOGUE.

As evening insects covet flame,
Do foolish men a little fame.

THE POET'S EPILOGUE.

I.

AUTUMN SONG.

In Spring the Poet is glad,
And in Summer the Poet is gay;
But in Autumn the Poet is sad,
And has something sad to say:

For the Wind moans in the Wood,
And the Leaf drops from the Tree;
And the cold Rain falls on the graves of the Good,
And the cold Mist comes up from the Sea:

And the Autumn Songs of the Poet's soul
Are set to the passionate grief,
Of Winds that sough and Bells that toll,
The Dirge of the Falling Leaf.

II.

THE ENEMY.

It was the dead
Of the long, long dark night;
And in my silent chamber the dim light
A pallid lustre shed.

Then with more care
Than is my wont withal,
I wended down the staircase, through the hall,
Into the open air.

And walked apart,
To feel the midnight spell;
And see if aught, perchance there were, not well,
Around my house and heart.

But by and by,
While yet I paced the court, —
As might the sentry of some sleeping fort, —
I heard a sudden cry.

And well aware
The Wolf was in the fold,
I sprang into my chamber: and behold,
Mine Enemy was there!

Dark eidolon!
As still as Death — agape,
Stretched at full length mid-floor, there was a Shape,
Which the lamp glared upon

But, at the touch,
As I strode on him right,
Lo, he was standing all at once his height,
And I was in his clutch!

On the bare bone
Did seem to shift and slide
The serpent-supple skin; and the ribbed side
Did grate against my own.

Each eye of flame
Glared as from some deep delf;
And he did cleave as if to crush himself
Into this mortal frame.

And I, to check,
Could then but straightway cast
Around his bony shoulders, and make fast
Unto his gaunt crook-neck.

And a strange strength
Did suddenly involve
And string my sinews with seven-fold resolve—
To conquer him at length!

But his close fold
He tightened; and did make
Fierce and terrific writhings, as to break
Mine unrelinquished hold.

But at its worth,
I clave to mine intent;
And at the first faint sign that he was spent,
Did straightway drag him forth.

God give us grace!
Forthwith each bony beak
Of his gaunt chin, and jaw, and hollow cheek,
Were thrust into my face!

But as before,
Was strength vouchsafed to check, —
And vantage still, by chance of his death's-neck,
To hale him down to door.

Then he did strain
His last; and in the wrench,
Off brake the skull-head to its socket's clench!
I hurled it forth amain!

And it did bowl
And bump the curb ! and sheer,
The Headless headlong, down, did disappear !—
And Peace came to my Soul !

And naught could chafe
Or chide me as I knelt
Beside my glimmering couch, at length, and felt
That my Beloved were safe.

And at first beam
Of morn without, did dawn
A sunrise in my senses : The foregone
Had vanished like a dream.

Then I did sing :
" Love, thou hast strength to save !
Hosanna, Lord ! Where is thy Victory, Grave ?
O Death, where is thy sting ? "

III.

THE LAST WATCH.

I.

The stars shine down through the shivering boughs,
And the moonset sparkles against the spire·
There is not a light in a neighbor's house,
Save one that burneth low,
And seemeth almost spent!
With shadowy forms in dark attire
Flickering in it to and fro,
As if in Pain and Doubt—
And heads bowed down in tears!
Hark!
Was there not Lament?—
Behold, behold the Light burns out!
The Picture disappears!

II.

Ye who with such sleepless sleight,
In the chamber out of sight,

Whispering low,
To and fro,
Your swift needles secretly
At the dead of night do ply, —
What is it that ye sew!

III.

"Hark! Hark!
Heard ye not the sounds aloof,
As of winds or wings that swept the roof?
Band of heavenly voices blending,
Choir of seraphim ascending?
Hark! Hark!"

IV.

"Away! Away!
Behold, behold it is the day!
Bear her softly out of the door;
And upward, upward, upward soar!"

IV.

L' INCORONATA.

Come, thou stillest of all Hours,
  Let abroad go nothing ill;
That the Vestals of the Flowers
  May their mystic rites fulfil.

On her brow is set the splendor
  Of the Everlasting Seal;
And behold the Vestals enter,
  And around The Maiden kneel!

Slowly as sweet incense stealing
  Upward on the Sabbath air,
All arising from their kneeling,
  Take the flowers from their hair

Noiseless-footed, odor-breathing,
  Azure-bodied, vapor-slow, —
All around and round her wreathing, —
  Doth the lovely Chorus go!

None with weeping, none with grieving, —
Being pure forevermore! —
What are they so fondly weaving
Of the Flowers which they wore?

'T is the Wreath!
'T is the Heavenly Wreath!
'T is the Wreath of the Heart's Desire,
'T is the Wreath of the Vestal Choir!
'T is the Vestal Wreath.

"Twine! Vestal Sisters! Twine!
All in sweetest surety;
Twine the Valley-Lily's bells
With Maidenhair, and Immortelles,
And all the Flowers of Purity, —
Vestal Sisters, twine and twine!

"Round and round the virgin brow,
Holy keep the Vestal Vow!

Sacred keep the Vestal Spell:
Weave it deep and weave it well!
Weave it sweet and weave it sure!
Blessed, blessed are the Pure.

"Twine! Twine!
Sisters, ere the moon is set,
Twine the white, White Violet,—
While the Vestal dews are on it yet,—
With the myriad-starréd Mignonette;
Twine, Vestal Sisters, twine!

"Hand to hand around her head,
With a blossom-light, slow tread!
Leaf to leaf, and stem to stem,
Weave the Vestal Diadem!—
Crescent, Crown, and Cynosure:
Blessed, blessed are the Pure.

"And twine, twine, twine,
The Fairest of all the Vestal Flowers,

That bloom in the blessed Eden-bowers
Of the Heart below, or the Heaven above:
The Maiden Flower of The Maiden's Love!
Twine, Vestal Sisters, twine!

"Crownéd is the virgin brow!
Holy kept the Vestal Vow!
Sacred kept the Vestal Spell:
She is crowned and crownéd well!
Crownéd sweet and crownéd sure!
Blessèd, blessed are the Pure."

V.

NO MORE.

This is the Burden of the Heart,
  The Burden that it always bore:
We live to love; we meet to part;
  And part to meet on earth No More:
We clasp each other to the heart,
  And part to meet on earth No More.

There is a time for tears to start, —
  For dews to fall and larks to soar:
The Time for Tears, is when we part
  To meet upon the earth No More:
The Time for Tears, is when we part
  To meet on this wide earth — No More.

VI.

LA SCINTILLA.

"I LIE in the shadow of the Earth,"
Said I to my Soul,
"In the depths of mine abysmal birth;
And the Darkness is deep on my house and my hearth:
There is not a star, — there is not a spark, —
And my life it is exceeding dark,
My life is very dark."

"O say not so! O say not so!"
(Said the Voice of my Soul,)
"For the Dawn will come and the Night will go:
Nay, nay, there is even now a glow
On the vast Altar of the Night, —
There 's a glimpse of the coming Light,
A gleam of the Heavenly Light!"

"It is the mock-light of a dream!"
Said I to my Soul,
"The torch-wraith of the marish stream,
Or only the dying glow-worm's gleam!—
My Hearth is cold and my Altar stark,
The earth is cold and the heavens are dark,
All dark,—all cold and dark."

"O say not so! O say not so!"—
(Said the Voice of my Soul,)
And she spake in a tone as sweet and low
As the first faint murmur and lapse and flow
Of the dawning Day to the dying Night,
"Behold, there is even now a Light—
A little Spark of Light!"

"Alas, dear Soul, and alas for me!"
Said I to my Soul,
"Alas, for an eye that cannot see,
And alas, for a bliss that can never be!
'T is but the phosphor's fitful spark

That will vanish away and leave it dark,
And leave it just as dark."

"O nay! For it surely is not so!"
(Said the Voice of my Soul,)
And the wreath of an arm as white as snow
Was woven around me! And lo, and lo!
As she spake, it came in sight!
And behold, it was the Living Light,
A Spark of the Living Light!

"Is it the gleam and the glamoury,"
Said I to my Soul,
"Of a starry Eyebeam that I see?
O tell me, — what? — what can it be?"
And I looked again: and behold, The Spark
Shone out like a little face in the dark,
Like a Little Face in the dark!

"O it is not an eye-beam that we see,"
Said the Voice of my Soul!

"But the Beam of The Little Soul," said she,
"That is gone to its Immortality!
And that cometh down at the dead of The Night,
To guide us up to the Gates of Light,
To the Fountain-head of Light!"

"Then Come! and with it let us go!"
Said I to my Soul:
And she raised me up in her arms of snow!
And the Darkness vanished in a glow
Of rapture unspeakable from our sight!
And the Universe was a flood of Light,
Of Harmony and Light!

VII.

THE VOICE.

A SAINTLY Voice fell on my ear
Out of the dewy atmosphere:
"O hush, dear Bird of Night, be mute;
Be still, O throbbing heart and lute!"
The Night-Bird shook the sparkling dew
Upon me as he ruffed and flew;
My heart was still, almost as soon,
My lute as silent as the moon:
I hushed my heart, and held my breath,
And would have died the death of death,
To hear, — but just once more, — to hear
That Voice within the atmosphere.

Again The Voice fell on my ear,
Out of the dewy atmosphere!
The same words, but half heard at first, —
I listened with a quenchless thirst;

And drank as of that heavenly balm,
The Silence that succeeds a psalm:
My soul to ecstasy was stirred:
It was a Voice that I had heard
A thousand blissful times before;
But deemed that I should hear no more
Till I should have a Spirit's ear,
And breathe another Atmosphere!

Then there was Silence in my ear,
And Silence in the atmosphere;
And silent moonshine on the mart,
And Peace and Silence in my heart;
But suddenly a dark Doubt said:
"The fancy of a fevered head!"
A wild, quick whirlwind of desire
Then wrapt me as in folds of fire:
I ran the strange words o'er and o'er,
And listened breathlessly once more:
And lo, the third time, I did hear
The same words in the atmosphere!

They fell and died upon my ear,
As dew dies on the atmosphere:
And then an intense yearning thrilled
My Soul, that all might be fulfilled:
"Where art thou, Blessed Spirit, where?
Whose Voice is dew upon the air!"
I looked, around me, and above,
And cried aloud: "Where art thou, Love?
O let me see thy living eye,
And clasp thy living hand, or die!"
Again, upon the atmosphere,
The self-same words fell: "*I Am Here.*"

"Here? Thou art here, Love!" "*I Am Here:*"
The echo died upon my ear:
I looked around me — everywhere;
But Ah! there was no mortal there!
The moonlight was upon the mart,
And Awe and Wonder in my heart!

I saw no form!—I only felt
Heaven's Peace upon me as I knelt:
And knew a Soul Beatified
Was at that moment by my side!
And there was Silence in my ear,
And Silence in the atmosphere!

VIII.

I SAID TO THE ROSE.

I SAID to the Rose,
"Thy Palace close,
For the Summer is gone before!"
I said to the Lark,
"The Night is dark,
And the Morning will come no more!"

But behold, behold,
From the Misty Fold,
That beautiful Image seems,
With lifted veil,
To give me "Hail,"
And to beckon me Home in dreams!

And again the hush
Of my heart is a flush

And a flood of glad refrains!
    And the dying Night
    Is wrapt in a white,
Strange death-sheet of sweet strains!

THE END.

Cambridge: Stereotyped and Printed by Welch, Bigelow, & Co.

CPSIA information can be obtained
at www.ICGtesting.com
Printed in the USA
LVHW041924090322
713000LV00004B/457

9 783752 575620